WIGGLESBOTTOM PRIMARY

DINO CHICK

PAMELA
BUTCHART

nosy crow

BECKA
MOOR

WELCOME TO WIGGLESBOTTOM PRIMARY!

MISS RILEY

HANA

LAUREN

JAYDEN

IRFAN

EVIE

MEGAN

MILES

SUSIE

MR HARRIS

ROZ

SUNITA

GAVIN

JOEL

ANNE-MARIE

BOBBY

THEO

First published in 2021 by Nosy Crow Ltd
The Crow's Nest, 14 Baden Place,
Crosby Row, London SE1 1YW

www.nosycrow.com

ISBN: 978 1 83994 071 2

Printed in Spain

Papers used by Nosy Crow are made from wood grown in
sustainable forests.

1 3 5 7 9 10 8 6 4 2

CONTENTS

For Ali Harris
and her daddy x
P. B.

For Hank and Martha
B. M.

DINO
CHICK

On Monday, when we got to class, Miss Riley said that she had a **SURPRISE** for us. And then she pointed to a big glass box that looked a bit like a **FISH TANK**. And that's when we all **CHEERED** and Jayden King said that it was the

BEST DAY OF HIS LIFE

because we all thought we were getting a **CLASS FISH**.

But that's when Miss Riley said that it **WASN'T** a fish tank and that it was an **INCUBATOR**.

We didn't know what an **INCUBATOR** was so Miss Riley took us over to it and pointed and that's when we saw that there were **FOUR EGGS** inside and she told us that they were **CHICKEN EGGS** and that the **INCUBATOR** kept the eggs nice and warm until the chicks **HATCHED**.

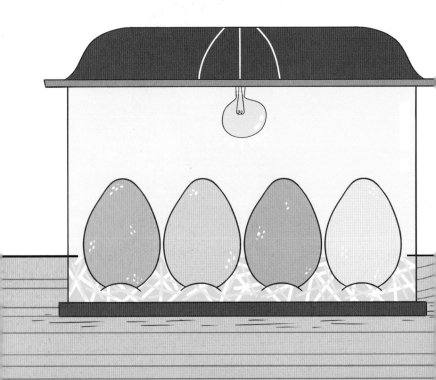

That's when Jayden King **GASPED** and said,

"We're getting

BABY

CHICKS!"

And Miss Riley smiled and nodded and we all

CHEERED

louder than when we thought it was **FISH** because **CHICKS** are even better than fish!

So we all

STARED

at the **EGGS** because we couldn't **WAIT** for one of them to hatch.

But then Miss Riley made us all sit down because she said that the eggs weren't going to hatch that very minute and that it could take

DAYS.

But then after lunch, Theo said that he was a bit **WORRIED** about one of the eggs because it had

CHANGED

COLOUR.

And we all looked and saw that one of the eggs was now **PURPLE** and **GREEN** with **SQUIGGLY LINES** all over it.

So we all ran and got Miss Riley and when she saw the egg she looked

SHOCKED.

That's when she made us all sit down and told us to

LISTEN VERY CAREFULLY

and she even used her **STERN VOICE** so we knew that this was **SERIOUS**.

Miss Riley said that the eggs were **NOT TOYS** and that we had to be **EXTRA CAREFUL** around them and that

UNDER NO CIRCUMSTANCES
should we touch any of them.

We had

NO IDEA

what was going on or why the **EGG** had changed colour or why Miss Riley looked so upset. But then, at break, Megan McNally said that she knew **EXACTLY** what was going on and that the purple and green egg **WASN'T** a chicken egg and that it was obviously a

DINOSAUR EGG.

Megan said that that was why Miss Riley had looked so **SHOCKED** when she saw it and told us to be **EXTRA CAREFUL** and not to **TOUCH IT** because she was **SCARED**.

That afternoon, **NO ONE** could take their eyes off the egg because we were all **TERRIFIED** that it was going to **HATCH** before the end-of-day bell. But it didn't.

And then on Tuesday **NO ONE** would go inside the classroom until we were **SURE** the egg hadn't hatched overnight in case there was a **DINOSAUR** loose in the classroom.

So we all took turns **WATCHING** the egg but nothing happened on Tuesday.

And nothing happened on Wednesday either.

And by Thursday we were beginning to think the eggs were **NEVER** going to hatch.

But then, before lunch, Jayden King **SQUEALED**,

"**THE EGGS ARE MOVING!**"

So we all **RUSHED** over to the incubator and that's when we saw that the eggs were **SHAKING** a bit.

That's when Miles McKay said that it was **ONLY A MATTER OF TIME** before the eggs hatched and we had a **REAL LIVE DINOSAUR** on our hands.

After lunch, when we got back to the classroom, Miss Riley said that she had **BIG NEWS** and then she pointed to the incubator and we saw that there were **THREE BABY CHICKS**.

But the **DINO EGG** still hadn't hatched.
Miss Riley said that she was a bit
WORRIED about the last egg but that
all we could do was **WAIT AND SEE**.

We all **STARED** at each other when she
said that because we knew that Miss Riley
was worried because she knew it was a
DINO EGG and that there was probably
a baby **T-REX** with loads of **SHARP
TEETH** inside!

Then all of a sudden the **DINO EGG** started to

WOBBLE.

And a

CRACK

appeared in the shell and Miss Riley **GASPED**.

And then we **ALL** gasped because the egg cracked again and a **TOOTH** came poking out!

That's when Susie Keys **SQUEALED** and ran out of the classroom and Miss Riley ran after her.

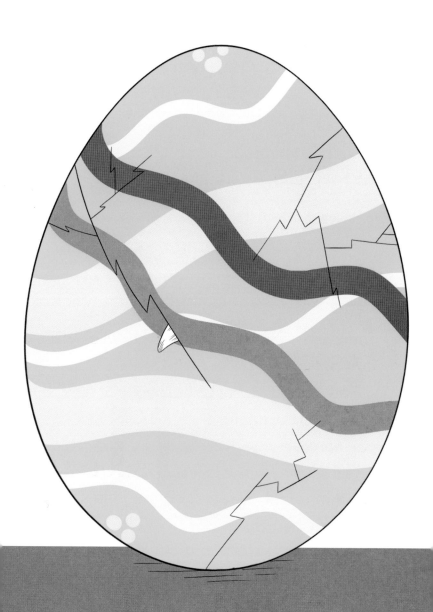

Sunita Ram said that we should all take a **STEP BACK** and that we should do it **REALLY SLOWLY**.

Then Joel Jack said that we should **HOLD HANDS** around the incubator to **SUPPORT** each other because this was **SERIOUS**. So we did.

But then all of a sudden the rest of the **DINO EGG** cracked open and that's when we saw that the tooth **WASN'T** a tooth because it was a **BEAK**. And that it belonged to a tiny, fluffy chick! That's when Miss Riley came rushing back in with Susie and said, "Is everything **OK**? Did it hatch?!"

So we all started yelling that everything was **OK** and that it **WASN'T** a dinosaur

after all and that it was another **BABY CHICK** and that we were all safe!

Miss Riley looked a bit confused. So we explained about the egg changing colour and about how she had given us a **TALK** about being **EXTRA CAREFUL** with the eggs and not to **TOUCH** them. And how we thought this was because the purple and green one was a **DINO EGG**.

And that's when Miss Riley said that the reason she'd given us a **TALK** was because someone had taken the egg out of the **INCUBATOR** and **DECORATED** it in **PEN**. And then she gave Susie Keys a bit of a look and Susie looked down at the ground and said sorry and that she'd just been trying to make the eggs look **PRETTY** because she **LOVED THEM SO MUCH**.

Then Miss Riley said that she'd been a bit worried about the egg and that it might not hatch because the eggs are not supposed to be taken out of the incubator and that you are definitely not supposed to draw on them in pen.

But then Miss Riley smiled and said, "But never mind about that now because **LOOK**! All of the eggs have hatched and the chicks are **SUPER CUTE!**"

EVERYONE was excited about the chicks and we all wanted to hold them and give them names.

But then one of the chicks opened its beak **REALLY WIDE** and did a **TINY ROAR**. And its eyes seemed to **GLOW RED** for a moment.

We all looked at each other and **GASPED**.

But then when we looked back at the chick it had its beak closed and was cheeping and looking all cute and fluffy and normal-eyed.

But we **KNEW**.

It **WAS** a **DINO CHICK!**

THE NEW GIRL

One day, when we were doing our maths, there was a knock at the classroom door.

That's when we all stopped doing our maths **RIGHT AWAY** and looked up and saw that it was one of the **OFFICE LADIES**.

We all knew that something was about to happen because when an office lady comes to your door it's usually about

SOMETHING BIG.

Theo Burke **GASPED** and said that he thought we were all about to get **SENT HOME** because of

HEAD LICE

and that's when **EVERYONE** gasped and started scratching their heads

LOADS.

But then the door opened and we saw that there was someone **ELSE** standing next to the office lady and we all **STARED** because it was a **GIRL** and she looked about the same age as us but **NONE OF US** had ever seen her before!

That's when Miss Riley said, "Hello! Come in! Come in!"

And then she turned to us and said, "Everyone! This is Ali. She'll be joining our class. Please give her a great big Class **2R** welcome!"

We all **STARED** at Miss Riley with our mouths **WIDE OPEN** because we had

NO IDEA

we were getting a **NEW PUPIL** and also because we didn't know **HOW** to welcome one because this had **NEVER** happened to us before!

Then all of a sudden, Joel Jack stood up and started clapping, really loud. So that's when we all stood up and did the same and Ali smiled loads and Miss Riley started laughing. **EVERYONE** wanted to speak to the

NEW GIRL

and sit next to her and be the one to be in **CHARGE** of her. But Miss Riley said that we needed to calm down a bit and let Ali **SETTLE IN** and stop asking her **ONE HUNDRED QUESTIONS**.

But that was hard because we didn't know **ANYTHING** about her, like what her favourite colour was, or what the school dinners were like at her old school or who she wanted to be **BEST FRIENDS** with.

We all **HELD OUR BREATH** when Miss Riley took the extra chair out of the store cupboard and watched closely to see which table she was going to put it down at.

Then Miss Riley walked over to the **BLUE** table and put it down next to Sunita Ram and Sunita yelled, "**YES!**" really loud and punched the air with her fist.

43

At break, Sunita said that she was going to show Ali around the **WHOLE SCHOOL**. But Jayden King said that that **WASN'T FAIR** and that we needed to split the school up so that **EVERYONE** got a turn to show the

NEW GIRL around.

So that's what we did, and when it was my turn I got to show Ali the first set of stairs that go up to the top floor and Theo Burke got to show her the second set.

But then Ali stopped smiling and she looked a bit sad so that's when Theo said that he was going to show her somewhere that was **OUT OF BOUNDS** and we all **GASPED** and Ali's eyes went **WIDE**.

Then all of a sudden, Theo shouted,

"FOLLOW ME!"

and then he **RAN** all the way to the **STAFF ROOM**.

47

That's when Theo said that he was going to open the **DOOR** so Ali could see inside and we all **GASPED** because that is **NOT ALLOWED**.

We all **STARED** as Theo opened the door **REALLY SLOWLY** and let Ali peek inside.

And Ali said,

"COOL!"

So that's when Roz Morgan said **SHE** was taking Ali somewhere

MORE COOL

and then she grabbed Ali's hand and ran all the way to the **STAFF TOILET** and said she was "**GOING IN**".

NONE of us thought that Roz was **ACTUALLY** going to do it. Because the staff toilet is even more

OUT OF BOUNDS

than the staff room!

So we couldn't **BELIEVE IT** when Roz opened the door and ran inside! And I couldn't stop thinking about what it looked like in there and if there were loads of fancy **CANDLES** and **LAMPS** and maybe even a **RUG**.

Then all of a sudden the door burst open and Roz **RUSHED** out holding a **PAPER TOWEL** and handed it to Ali, and Ali smiled loads and said, "**AWESOME!**"

But then we heard a toilet flush and someone shouted, "**RUN!**" and we ran away.

And **THAT'S** when everything started to get **OUT OF CONTROL** because Irfan Baxter said that he was going to take Ali to see the most **OUT OF BOUNDS** thing in the **WHOLE SCHOOL EVER**.

Then he smiled and said, "I'm going to take Ali to see the head teacher's **CAR**. And I'm going to **TOUCH IT**."

And that's when everyone **GASPED** because Mr Harris is **VERY SERIOUS** about his car, and he doesn't even park it in the car park beside the other cars, he parks it on the grass right next to his office so he can watch it from his window.

I didn't think touching the head teacher's car sounded like a very good **IDEA** but before any of us could do **ANYTHING** Irfan ran outside and over to Mr Harris's car and put his **FULL HAND** on it!

So we all started **COUNTING** to see how long Irfan would keep his hand on Mr Harris's car and we got all the way to **EIGHT**. But then the bell rang and Irfan **SCREAMED** and we all ran away.

55

When we got back to class, **EVERYONE** was

FREAKING OUT

and saying that Irfan was going to get

EXPELLED

because there was **CCTV** and that Mr Harris watched it **ALL THE TIME** and that the **POLICE** would probably be here soon.

And that's when Ali **LAUGHED** even though it wasn't funny at **ALL**.

But then all of a sudden Miss Riley handed Ali a new **TRAY** and when we saw it we all **GASPED** because Miss Riley puts our first **AND** second names on our trays. And Ali's said: **ALI HARRIS**.

We all **GASPED** because she had the same second name as Mr Harris!

That's when Ali did a **WEIRD SMILE** and Sunita said, "Is Mr Harris your **DAD**?!" And Ali nodded.

And we all looked at each other because **THAT'S** when we knew that we were all going to get

EXPELLED FOR LIFE

because we'd taken the head teacher's daughter to the **STAFF ROOM** and the

STAFF TOILET

and we'd even touched the

HEAD TEACHER'S CAR!

Then Irfan said, "If we'd known you were the head teacher's daughter we wouldn't have done any of that!"

And he started **BEGGING** Ali not to tell her dad and she smiled and said she **DEFINITELY** wouldn't and that she was actually really **NERVOUS** about being here because her dad was the head teacher and that she was worried that people wouldn't want to be friends with her because they were too **SCARED** of her.

That's when Ali said that it had felt **GREAT** to be involved in all the

RULE

BREAKING

and that it made her feel like she was

ONE
OF
US.

So that's when we told her that she **WAS** one of us and also that we don't normally break the rules and that we'd only been doing it to **CHEER HER UP** because she'd looked a bit sad.

And we said that we all really **LIKED** her dad and that he was a great head teacher because he **IS** and that made her really happy.

But then Mr Harris appeared at the door and he had a bit of a weird look on his face and that's when Ali whispered to us, "I think he's just worried about me. I think he needs a cuddle."

So we all peeked through the glass and saw Mr Harris getting a cuddle from Ali and they both looked really happy.

Then when Ali came back, Irfan said, "Do you think because your dad is the head teacher you could maybe talk to him about us getting chocolate ice cream at school dinners?"

And Ali winked and said, "Maybe!"
And we all cheered.

THE CUPCAKE CAPER

It all started on Monday when we found the librarian, Mr Hope, sitting on the floor behind his desk. And he was **CRYING** and eating a family-sized bag of **CRISPS**.

That's when we found out that Mr Hope was crying because he'd just been told that he couldn't be our librarian any more because the library was

CLOSING FOR EVER.

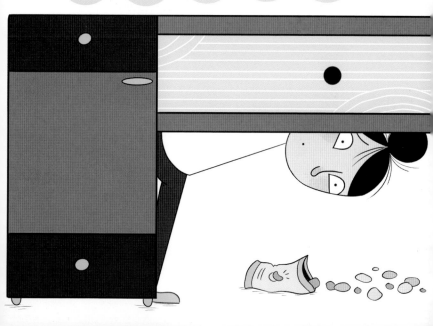

We were all

SHOCKED

because it didn't make any **SENSE** to shut the school library because that's where all the **BOOKS** are!

Mr Hope said that it had to do with

SCHOOL FUNDS

and that the school didn't have enough money to have a library any more.

We were all really upset about not having a library any more and Jayden King said that he was actually **ANGRY** about it and that it wasn't **FAIR** and that he hadn't even **LIKED** reading until Mr Hope helped him find books that were actually **GOOD** and that now he'd read over **FIFTY** books!

That's when Joel Jack said that he didn't think it was fair **EITHER** and that he wanted to have an

EMERGENCY
MEETING

about it all

ASAP.

So we all ran behind the bike shed and sat down on the grass and waited to hear what Joel had to say.

Joel said that if the school didn't have enough **MONEY** to keep the **LIBRARY** open then it was

ONLY A MATTER OF TIME

before they started shutting **OTHER** parts of the school.

Like the

DINNER HALL

or the

PLAYGROUND

or even the

TOILETS.

But then Joel **SMILED** and said that he had a **PLAN** to save the **LIBRARY** and probably even the whole **SCHOOL**. And that he was calling his plan

THE CUPCAKE PLAN

because it had to do with cupcakes and us making **LOADS** of them and **SELLING** them to make money to keep the library **AND** the toilets open.

Everyone **CHEERED** when Joel said that because it was a

BRILLIANT

plan and we all **LOVE** cupcakes!

Joel said that we needed to go home and tell our mums and dads and carers about what was happening with the library and make as many cupcakes as **POSSIBLE**. And then we had to meet at the school

gates **FIRST THING** tomorrow to count how many we had and then take them to the **STAFF ROOM** and sell them to the teachers for **TEN POUNDS EACH** because the teachers all **LOVE** cake.

One time, when it was Miss Riley's **BIRTHDAY**, there was a **CAKE** and we actually heard

SQUEALING

coming from the staff room and loads of **LAUGHING** because they were all going **WILD** for the cake!

So that's what we did. And the next day when we got to school we sat on the grass next to the school gates and started to count how many cakes we had. And we had quite a **LOT** actually and there were even some homemade **BISCUITS** and **CRISPY CAKES**.

We were all really **EXCITED** and we were just about to go to the staff room when **JAYDEN KING** got out of a **BIG VAN** with his mum and dad and they were all carrying **HUGE BOXES** of cupcakes and none of us could **BELIEVE** how many they'd made!

That's when Jayden said that his mum and dad got so upset about the library closing that they'd stayed up **ALL NIGHT** making cupcakes and that they'd made

THREE

HUNDRED.

Then Joel Jack said we had so many that we should use them to spell out **SAVE OUR LIBRARY!** on the grass.

And that was a

BRILLIANT IDEA

so that's what we did.

That's when loads of **PARENTS** started to turn up at the school gates and they saw all the cupcakes. And suddenly there were **LOADS** of people there and they were all asking about the cupcakes.

Then all the teachers came outside and asked us what we were doing. So we explained about the library and Mr Hope and the **CUPCAKE PLAN**.

Then all of a sudden there was **ANOTHER** van but it wasn't more cupcakes, it was a lady from the **TV** and she had a **CAMERA** and a **CAMERA MAN** and a **MICROPHONE**.

EVERYONE was mega excited because we knew that we were going to be on the **TV** so we kept waving at the camera and holding up the cupcakes and Megan McNally even did a **BACK FLIP** with a cupcake in her mouth!

Then Mr Harris the head teacher came out and he looked **SHOCKED**. And we knew that it was because he'd never **SEEN** so many cupcakes in his **LIFE** and that he was **MEGA IMPRESSED**.

That's when the lady from the **TV** put the **MICROPHONE** in front of his face and asked him about closing the school library and about Mr Hope and all the **CUPCAKES**.

And that's when Mr Harris got a bit upset and said that it was a

MISTAKE

and that he was going to fight to get the funds to keep the library **OPEN** with Mr Hope in it. And that we could use the funds from the **CUPCAKES** to make **POSTERS** and start a **PETITION** and hire **FILMING EQUIPMENT** to make a **VIDEO** about saving the library to

SPREAD THE WORD.

And we all **CHEERED**.

But then Susie Keys **GASPED** and said, "You're not going to close the **TOILETS** instead, are you?!"

And that's when we all **GASPED** and the lady from the **TV** shoved the microphone back in front of Mr Harris's face.

But then Mr Harris said that he **WOULD NOT** be shutting the toilets **OR** anything else and that he was **PROUD** of us all for caring so much about our library. And that's when Mr Hope rushed over and he

wasn't crying any more and he gave Mr Harris a **HIGH FIVE** and we were all **SHOCKED** because we didn't know that Mr Harris knew how to do that!

Then we all cheered again and Sunita Ram handed Mr Harris a cupcake.

And once he started eating it she said, "That'll be ten pounds please!"

And that's when Mr Harris started **CHOKING** and we all had to pat him on the back.

And then when he finally stopped choking, Sunita put out her hand and said, "Ten pounds please!"